A Good Night's Sleep

This book belongs to:

....

The farming day
Is nearly done.

Tractor Ted and Midge
Had so much fun!

They milked the cows,

And fed some sheep.

They watched
piglets wallow

In **mud** knee deep!

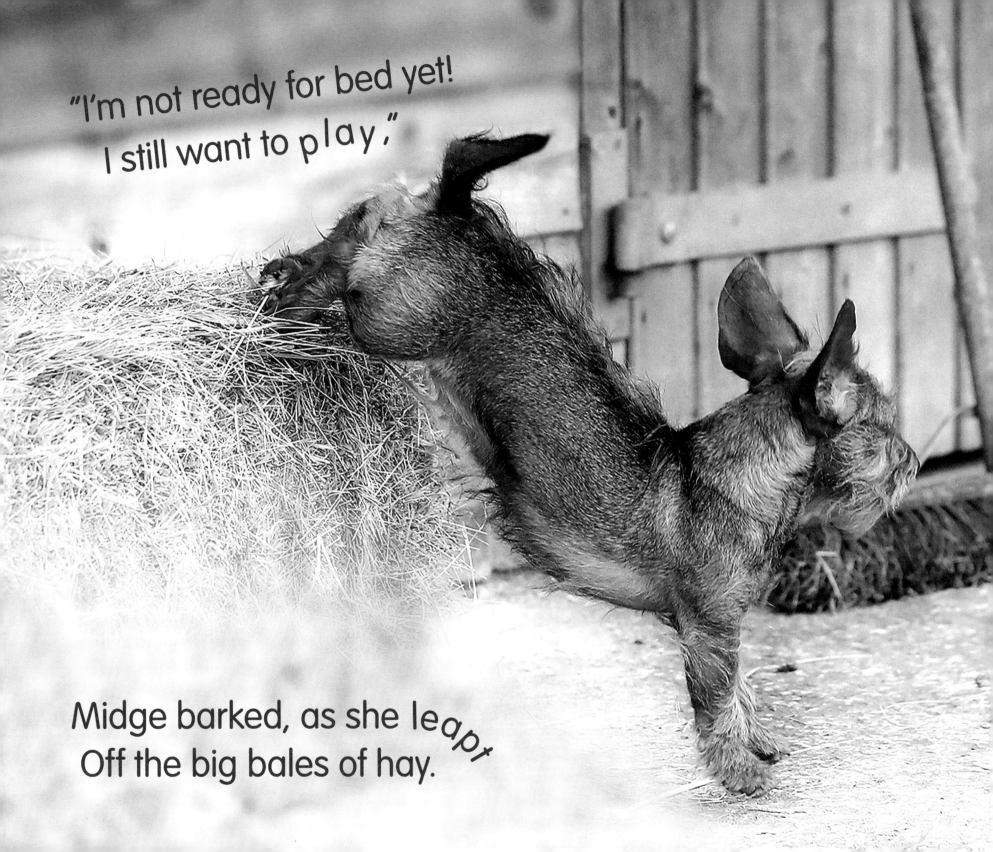

"But didn't you know
That sleep is good?

It helps your body
Grow as it should

"Look at the calves!
It won't be long,

With some sleep they will grow
To be **big** and **strong**.

"See how the chicks
In the nest are so small?

"With sleep they'll grow feathers
And lay eggs for us all."

Merlin said,
"Hmph,
You know
he is right.

"Your body needs rest
At the end of the day,

Then tomorrow you'll wake up
Ready to play.

"Soon the stars will be out
And so will the moon.

Let's go to bed
And I'll see you soon."

So Midge snuggled down
And closed her eyes tight.

She knew Tractor Ted

And Merlin were right.

Tractor Ted drove off
    To sleep in his barn.

He was tired from the
Busy day on the farm.

As everyone slept

The owl gave a hoot.

Tractor Ted said goodnight

With a quiet,

Toot toot.

TED 1